Percy B. Shelley

Letters from Percy Bysshe Shelley to Robert Southey

and other correspondents

Percy B. Shelley

Letters from Percy Bysshe Shelley to Robert Southey
and other correspondents

ISBN/EAN: 9783337388140

Printed in Europe, USA, Canada, Australia, Japan

Cover: Foto ©Andreas Hilbeck / pixelio.de

More available books at **www.hansebooks.com**

LETTERS

FROM

PERCY BYSSHE SHELLEY

TO

ROBERT SOUTHEY,

AND OTHER CORRESPONDENTS.

1886.

New York : Privately Printed.

(*Not for Sale.*)

" Most of the qualities of a good letter-writer were combined in Shelley, and Fortune also favoured the development of his genius in this direction. . . . . If that age [the nineteenth century] had any master of epistolary composition among its wonderful poets, it was Shelley : Shelley or none."

SHELLEY'S LETTERS.

LETTER I.

To Robert Southey.

Messrs. Longdill & Co.,
5, Gray's Inn Square,
March 7th, 1816.

My dear Sir,

I cannot refrain from presenting you with a little poem [Alastor], the product of a few serene hours of the last beautiful autumn. I shall never forget the pleasure which I derived from your conversation, or the kindness with which I was received in your hospitable circle during the short period of my stay in Cumberland some years ago. The disappointment of some youthful hopes, and subsequent misfortunes of a heavier nature, are all that I can plead as my excuse for neglecting to write to you, as I had promised, from Ireland. The true weight of this apology you cannot know. Let it be sufficient that, regarding you with admiration as a poet, and with respect as a man, I send you, as an intimation of those sentiments, my first serious attempt to interest the best feelings of the human heart, believing that you have so much general charity as to forget, like me, how widely in moral and political opinions we disagree, and to attribute that difference to better motives than the multitude are disposed to allege as the cause of dissent from their institutions.

Very sincerely yours,

Percy B. Shelley.

LETTER II.

·To Robert Southey.

Pisa,
June 26th, 1820.

Dear Sir,

Some friends of mine persist in affirming that you are the author of a criticism which appeared ·some time since in the *Quarterly Review* on the *Revolt of Islam.*

I know nothing that would give me more sincere pleasure than to be able.to affirm from your own assurance that you were not guilty of that writing. I confess I see such strong internal evidence against the charge, without reference to what I think I know of the generous sensibility of your character, that had

my own conviction only been concerned, I should never have troubled
you to deny what I firmly believe you
would have spurned to do.

Our short personal intercourse has
always been remembered by me with
pleasure ; and when I recalled the
enthusiasm with which I then con-
sidered your writings, with gratitude for
your notice, we parted, I think, with
feelings of mutual kindness. The
article in question, except in reference
to the possibility of its having been
written by you, is not worth a moment's
attention.

That an unprincipled hireling, in
default of what to answer in a published
composition, should, without provoca-
tion, insult over the domestic calamities
of a writer of the adverse party—to
which perhaps their victim dares scarce-
ly advert in thought—that he should
make those calamities the theme of the
foulest and the falsest slander—that all

this should be done by a calumniator without a name—with the cowardice, no less than the malignity, of an assassin—is too common a piece of charity among Christians (Christ would have taught them better), too common a violation of what is due from man to man among the pretended friends of social order, to have drawn one remark from me, but that I would have you observe the arts practised by that party for which you have abandoned the cause to which your early writings were devoted. I had intended to have called on you, for the purpose of saying what I now write, on my return to England ; but the wretched state of my health detains me here, and I fear leaves my enemy, were he such as I could deign to contend with, an easy, but a base victory, for I do not profess paper warfare. But there is a time for all things.

I regret to say that I shall consider

your neglecting to answer this letter a substantiation of the fact which it is intended to settle—and *therefore* I shall assuredly hear from you.

Dear sir, accept the best wishes of

Yours truly.

P. B. Shelley.

LETTER III.

To Robert Southey.

Pisa,
August 17*th*, 1820.

Dear Sir,

Allow me to acknowledge the sincere pleasure which I received from the first paragraph of your letter. The disavowal it contained was just such as I firmly anticipated.

Allow me also to assure you, that no menace implied in my letter could have the remotest application to yourself. I am not indeed aware that it contained any menace. I recollect expressing what contempt I felt, in the hope that you might meet the wretched hireling who has so closely imitated your style as to deceive all but those who knew you into a belief that he was you, at Murray's, or somewhere, and that you would inflict my letter on him, as a recompense for sowing ill-will between those who wish each other all good, as you and I do.

I confess your recommendation to adopt the system of ideas you call Christianity has little weight with me, whether you mean the popular superstition in all its articles, or some more refined theory with respect to those events and opinions which put an end to the graceful religion of the Greeks. To judge of the doctrines by their effects, one would think that this religion were called the religion of Christ and Charity, *ut lucus a non lucendo*, when I consider the manner in which they seem to have transformed the disposition and understanding of you and men of the most amiable manners and the highest accomplishments, so that even when recommending Christianity you cannot forbear

breathing out defiance against the
express words of Christ. What would
you have me think? You accuse me,
on what evidence I cannot guess, of
guilt—a bold word, sir, this, and one
which would have required me to write
to you in another tone, had you
addressed it to anyone except myself.
Instead, therefore, of refraining from
"judging that you be not judged," you
not only judge, but condemn, and that
to a punishment which its victim must
be either among the meanest or the
loftiest not to regard as bitterer than
death. But you are such a pure one
as Jesus Christ found not in all Judea
to throw the first stone against the
woman taken in adultery!

With what care do the most tyran-
nical courts of judicature weigh
evidence, and surround the accused
with protecting forms; with what re-
luctance do they pronounce their cruel
and presumptuous decisions compared

with you! You select a single passage
out of a life otherwise not only spotless
but spent in an impassioned pursuit of
virtue, which looks like a blot, merely
because I regulated my domestic ar-
rangements without deferring to the
notions of the vulgar, although I might
have done so quite as conveniently had
I descended to their base thoughts—
this you call *guilt*. I might answer
you in another manner, but I take God
to witness, if such a Being is now
regarding both you and me, and I
pledge myself if we meet, as perhaps
you expect, before Him after death, to
repeat the same in His presence—that
you accuse me wrongfully. I am
innocent of ill, either done or intended ;
the consequences you allude to flowed
in no respect from me. If you were
my friend, I could tell you a history
that would make you open your eyes ;
but I shall certainly never make the
public my familiar confidant.

You say you judge of opinions by the fruits ; so do I, but by their remote and permanent fruits—such fruits of rash judgment as Christianity seems to have produced in you. The immediate fruits of all new opinions are indeed calamity to the promulgators and professors ; but we see the end of nothing, and it is in acting well, in contempt of present advantage, that virtue consists.

I need not to be instructed that the opinion of the ruling party to which you have attached yourself always exacts, contumeliously receives, and never reciprocates, toleration. "But there is a tide in the affairs of men "— it is rising while we speak.

Another specimen of your Christianity is the judgement you form of the spirit of my verses, from the abuse of the Reviews. I have desired Mr. Ollier to send you those last published ; they may amuse you, for one of them—indeed, neither have anything to do with those speculations on which we differ.

I cannot hope that you will be candid enough to feel, or if you feel, to own, that you have done ill in accusing, even in your mind, an innocent and a persecuted man, whose only real offence is the holding opinions something similar to those which you once held respecting the existing state of society. Without this, further correspondence, the object for which I renewed it being once obtained, must, from the differences in our juggment, be irksome and useless. I hope some day to meet you in London, and ten minutes' conversation is worth ten folios of writing. Meanwhile assure yourself that, among all your good wishers, you have none who wish you better than, dear Sir,

Your very faithful and
Obedient servant,
P. B. SHELLEY.

P.S. I ought not to omit that I have had sickness enough, and that at this moment I have so severe a pain in the side that I can hardly write. All this is of no account in the favour of what you, or anyone else, calls Christianity ; surely it would be better to wish me health and healthful sensations. *I* hope the chickens will not come home to roost !

LETTER IV.

To Mr. Hitchener.

Nantgwillt, Rhayader,
Radnorshire, South Wales,
[*Thursday*] *April* 30*th*, 1812.

Sir,

I am your daughter's friend, of whom you may have heard her speak. You will consider it a sufficient introduction when *her* peace of mind is the subject of this intrusion.

The late letters which I have received from my friend have evinced considerable distress of mind, arising from reports circulated to the disadvantage of her reputation, which reports appear not to be without connexion with me and my little circle. It was not until we had determined on the plan of living together, of pursuing conjointly those avocations for which we had severally acquired a taste, that any of these calumnies reached her ears : and they would have passed unremarked by her and me, in the silence of merited contempt, if some infatuation had not gained them a sufficient degree of credit from you to disapprove of the plan on which we had determined.

Sir, my moral character is unimpeached and unimpeachable. I hate not calumny so much as I despise it. What the world thinks of my actions ever has, and I trust ever will be, a matter of the completest indifference. Your daughter shares this sentiment with me ; and we both are resolved to refer our actions to one tribunal only—that which Nature has implanted within us. I am married. My wife loves your daughter : she laughs at whatever the scandal of a few gossips out of employment might whisper, nor is she willing to sacrifice the inestimable society of her friend to the good opinion of the good people of Hurst or Horsham at the tea-party or card-table assembled. So far as myself and Mrs. Shelley are concerned, we are irrevocably resolved that no expedient shall be left untried on *our* part to induce our friend to share the prosperity or adversity of her lot with us.   Much as the strong affection which she bears you has prejudiced me in your favour, yet I would take my own opinion, particularly when it springs from my reasonings and feelings, before that of any man.   And you will forfeit the esteem I have thus acquired for your character if you endeavour by parental command to change the decisions of a free-born soul.

I understand that there is woven in the composition of your character a jealous watchfulness over the encroachments of those who happen to be born to more wealth and name than your-

self : you are perhaps right. It need
not be exerted now. *I* have no taste
for displaying genealogies, nor do I
wish to seem more important than
I am.

Yours sincerely,

P. B. SHELLEY.

LETTER V.

To Mr. Hitchener.

Nantgwillt, Rhayader,
Radnorshire, South Wales,
[*Thursday*] *May* 14*th*, 1812.

Sir,

If you have always considered *character* a possession of the first consequence, you and I essentially differ. If you think that an admission of your inferiority to the world leaves any corner by which yourself and character may aspire beyond its reach, we differ there again. In short, to be candid, I am deceived in my conception of your character.

I had some difficulty in stifling an indignant surprise on reading the sentence of your letter in which *you* refuse my invitation to your daughter. How

are you entitled to do this ? Who made
you her governor? Did you receive
this refusal from her, to communicate
to me? No, you have not. How are
you then constituted to answer a question which can only be addressed to
her ? Believe me, such an assumption
is as impotent as it is immoral. You
may cause your daughter much anxiety,
many troubles; you may stretch her
on a bed of sickness ; you may destroy
her body :—but you are defied to shake
her mind. She is now very ill. *You*
have agitated her mind until her frame
is seriously deranged. Take care, sir :
you may destroy her by disease, but her
mind is free : *that* you cannot hurt.

Your ideas of *propriety*—or, to express myself clearer, of *morals*—are
all founded on considerations of *profit.*
I do not mean money, but profit in
its extended sense.

As to your daughter's welfare,—in
that *she* is competent to judge; or at

least she alone has a right to decide.
With respect to your own comfort, you
of course do right to consult it : that
she has done so, you ought to be more
grateful than you appear.   But how
can you demand as a right what has been
generously conceded as a favour ? You
do right to consult your own comfort,
but the whole world besides may surely
be excused.   Neither the laws of Nature ·
nor of England have made children
private property.

Adieu.   When next I hear from you,
I hope that time will have liberalized
your sentiments.

Yours truly,

P. B. SHELLEY.

,LETTER VI.

To Hamilton Rowan.

Dublin,
7 Lower Sackville St.,
[*Tuesday*] *February* 25*th*, 1812.

Sir,

Although I have not the pleasure of being personally known to you, I consider the motives which actuated me in writing the enclosed sufficiently introductory to authorize me in sending you some copies, and waiving ceremonials in a case where public benefit is concerned. Sir, although an Englishman, I feel for Ireland; and I have left the country in which the chance of birth placed me, for the sole purpose of adding my little stock of usefulness to the fund which I hope that Ireland possesses to

aid her in the unequal yet sacred com-
bat in which she is engaged. In the
course of a few days more I shall print
another small pamphlet, which shall be
sent to you. I have intentionally vul-
garized the language of the enclosed.
I have printed 1500 copies, and am
now distributing them throughout
Dublin.

Sir, with respect,

I am your obedient humble servant,

P. B. SHELLEY.

LETTER VII.

TO THE
CHEVALIER JAMES DE LAURENCE.

LYNMOUTH, BARNSTAPLE, DEVON,
August 17*th,* 1812.

SIR,

I feel peculiar satisfaction in seizing the opportunity, which your politeness places in my power, of expressing to you (personally, as I may say) a high acknowledgment of my sense of your talents and principles, which, before I conceived it possible that I should ever know you, I sincerely entertained. Your *Empire of the Nairs,* which I read this spring, succeeded in making me a perfect convert to its doctrines. I then retained no doubts of the evils of marriage—Mrs. Wollstonecraft reasons too

well for that ; but I had been dull
enough not to perceive the greatest
argument against it, until developed in
the *Nairs*, viz : prostitution both *legal*
and *illegal.*

I am a young man not yet of age,
and have now been married a year to
a woman younger than myself. Love
seems inclined to stay in the " prison ; "
and my only reason for putting him in
chains, whilst convinced of the unholi-
ness of the act, was a knowledge that
in the present state of society, if Love
is not thus villainously treated, she who
is most loved will be treated worse by a
misjudging world.   In short, seduction,
which term could have no meaning
in a rational society, has now a most
tremendous one: the fictitious merit
attached to chastity has made *that* a
forerunner of the most terrible of ruins
which in Malabar would be a pledge
of honour and homage.   If there is any
enormous and desolating crime of

which I should shudder to be accused, it is seduction.

I need not say how much I admire *Love;* and, little as a British public seems to appreciate its merit, in never permitting it to emerge from a first edition, it is with satisfaction I find that justice has conceded abroad what bigotry has denied at home.

I shall take the liberty of sending you any little publication I may give to the world. Mrs. S. joins with me hoping, if we come to London this winter, we may be favoured with the personal friendship of one whose writings we have learned to esteem.

Yours very truly,
PERCY BYSSHE SHELLEY.

LETTER VIII.

To Mr. Hume.

Pisa,
February, 17*th,* 1820.

Sir,

I regret exceedingly that a mistake occasioned by a temporary pressure of affairs should have caused the annuity awarded to my children to have remained a quarter in arrear. If you will take the trouble to present the enclosed note to my friend Mr. Smith of the Stock Exchange any day after the 25th of March, that quarter, together with the quarter in arrear, will be paid ; and such measures are taken as will prevent any possible future misunderstanding on the subject.

Allow me to take this opportunity of

enquiring into the present state of the health and intellectual improve-ment of my children. I feel assured, although I have not the pleasure of a personal acquaintance with you, that you will excuse and comply with this request of a father who is the victim of the unexampled oppression of being for-bidden the exercise of his parental duties ; suffering in his own person the violation of those rights and those ties which until this instance the fiercest religious persecutions had ever con-sidered sacred. I only advert to my own wrongs—for the hour of redress is yet to arrive—that I may anticipate the gratitude which I shall owe to yourself and Mrs. Hume for the kindness and attention with which you doubtless perform all those (duties I can hardly call them) to my unfortunate children, except those which none but a parent can perform. I doubt not when they shall be restored to me but that the period which they have spent under your care will be remembered both by them and by me as having in some degree softened the inevitable ill of this unnatural separation.

Pray render acceptable to Mrs. Hume my best compts.

I remain, Sir,

Your obliged and obedient servant,

PERCY B. SHELLEY.

LETTER IX.

To William Laing.

London,
September, 27*th,* 1815.

Mr. William Laing,
Bookseller, Edinburgh.

Sir,

On unpacking the books which arrived from Edinburgh, I discover the following have been omitted, doubtless thro' mistake:

Drummond's *Academical Questions.*
Euripides *Hippolytus* (Marsh.)
Euripides *Heraclida Elmslen.*
Hoogeran *de Porticulis.*
I should feel myself much obliged if

you would send these books, which
have undoubtedly been mislaid and
confounded with yours—addressed to
me at Mr. Hookham, Old Bond
Street.

Your obedient Servt.

P. B. SHELLEY.

LETTER X.

26 MARCHMONT STREET,
BRUNSWICK SQUARE,
April 24th, 1816.

DEAR SIR,

In reply to the proposal made by you some months since to me on the part of Dr. Bethune, I wrote the other day to say that I would sell him the reversion at a fair price. In answer to your request as to the nature of the title I can convey accept the following statement. The estates of which this of Dr. Bethune is a part are given, by settlements dated August 1791, to my father for life to me in remainder. On my father's death by recovery I obtain the fee of these estates. I can make a deed which shall be binding upon myself in case I survive my father, and which shall be binding upon my infant son if I do not survive my father, either to alienate any particular estate, or to pay a certain sum of money. I have levied a fine and acquired this power, which I believe is called a *base fee*, which as I have before stated I am fully competent to convey. If I and my infant son should die before my father the security falls to the ground. But Dr. B. or any person might insure my life against my father's to whatever amount he should be beneficially interested. He need sustain *no loss in any case ;* and would only fail in his object of obtaining possession of the farm in question, if, what is very improbable, my father should survive not only me, but both myself and my infant son.

Dear Sir,
Your very obliged servant,
PERCY B. SHELLEY.